PAIR-IT BOOKS®

Schools Around the World

Written by Donald Mitchell

STECK-VAUGHN
ELEMENTARY · SECONDARY · ADULT · LIBRARY

A Harcourt Classroom Education Company

www.steck-vaughn.com

Peru

We walk to school.

China

We wear uniforms at school.

Japan

Our school is in a city.

Nepal

Our school is outside.

 5

Kenya

Our school has a grass roof.

Indonesia

Our school has no walls.

Venezuela

We have gym class inside.

China

We learn new games outside.

 9

Ecuador

We visit a palace on a field trip.

Germany

We go on a hike.

 11

Peru

We write on a chalkboard.

Nepal

We practice math together.

We learn to read together.

Honduras

We learn to write together.

U.S.A.

We all learn from each other.